In the Ghost Detective Universe:

Novels
(Best to be read in order)
Beyond the Grave
Unveiling the Past
Beneath the Surface
Piercing the Veil

Short Stories
(All stand-alone)
Just Desserts
Lost Friends
Family Bonds
Common Ground
Till Death
Family History
Heritage
New Beginnings
Far From Home
Severed Ties
Eternal Bond
Harsh Expectations
Dull Expectations

Short Story Collections
Unfinished Business, Volume 1
Unfinished Business, Volume 2

R.W. WALLACE

Author of *Beyond the Grave*

FAR FROM HOME

A Ghost Detective Short Story

Far From Home
by R.W. Wallace

Copyright © 2022 by R.W. Wallace

Cover by R.W. Wallace
Cover Illustration 10926765 © germanjames | 123rf.com
Cover Illustration 9181797 © jadthree | Depositphotos
Cover Illustration 192365728 © Natallia Haidutskaya | Dreamstime

This story was first published in *Pulphouse Fiction Magazine*, Issue #18

All characters and events in this book, other than those clearly in the public domain, are fictitious and any resemblance to real persons, living or dead, is purely coincidental.

All rights reserved. No part of this publication may be reproduced, distributed, or transmitted in any form or by any means, including photocopying, recording, or other electronic or mechanical methods, without the prior written permission of the publisher, except in the case of brief quotations embodied in critical reviews and certain other noncommercial uses permitted by copyright law. For permission requests, write to the publisher at the address below.

www.rwwallace.com

ISBN paperback: [978-2-493670-18-2]
ISBN ebook: [978-2-493670-19-9]

First edition

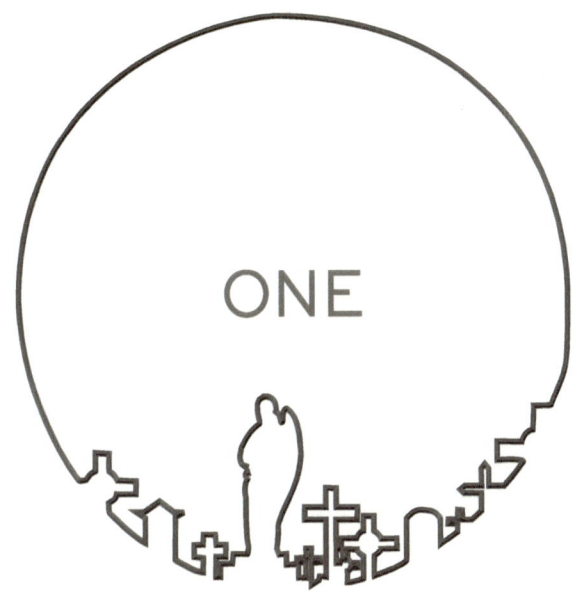

ONE

A CERTAIN PART of me is happy when someone becomes a ghost. It's not something I'm proud of, but I'm self-aware enough to know it's true.

See, when someone becomes a ghost, it's because they have unfinished business, so it's not exactly a good sign. For them. Especially because finishing said business when you're a ghost confined to a cemetery isn't always easy.

I can attest to that myself.

I've been a resident of this cemetery for over thirty years. My unfinished business is atoning for past sins, and I'm atoning by helping others find their peace. In real life I put bad guys in jail.

In the afterlife I teach ghosts about the keys to reach whatever awaits beyond the veil.

Basically, for me, it's a good thing if they're not at peace when they come here. I just need to not focus too hard on the egoistical part of that statement.

Of course, a new ghost also means company.

Now, I'm not exactly alone in this little cemetery. I haunt these hallowed grounds accompanied by my friend Clothilde. She has been here as long as I have and her key to deliverance is as elusive as mine. So despite our apparent differences, we've become close friends.

But years with only one companion can become a little restrictive, no matter how strong the friendship.

So when we hear the screams emanating from the bright white casket as the church doors open after the service, we both perk up.

A new arrival.

Sometimes we hang out by the church when there's a funeral, breathlessly—pun intended, we haven't drawn breath since we died—waiting to see if we'll have company. Other times, like today, we hang out on our own graves.

I blame the weather. Even though we can't feel the temperatures, it's obviously a cool spring morning, with a clear blue sky sporting a single bright white cloud just above the church spire, birds singing in the cypress trees by the main path, and bees buzzing in the wisteria on the north wall.

Lounging seems like a requirement.

So here I am, my ass parked on the small bump in the ground

marking my last resting place, leaning back on my arms, and my legs stretched before me, ankles crossed.

Clothilde is in her usual spot, perching on her gravestone, her hands under her jeans-clad legs, her Converse-covered feet dangling right through the stone. Her youthful face is turned away from me, her expression distant. My theory is that spring is a difficult time for Clothilde because it reminds her of how her life was cut too short—but I'd never discuss such a subject with her. It would earn me an eye roll or a scathing insult. Or possibly both.

Reading into things just isn't Clothilde's style.

Today's funeral procession is a large one. I'm guessing the nice weather had its effect on the number of people who decided to show up, but whoever is screaming his head off in that casket was definitely popular.

Clothilde and I join the mourners as they approach the newly dug grave. Whoever's in there has unfinished business, which means we need to help him finish it. Possibly help him discover what it is. And the people who decided to accompany him to his final resting place may have important information. So we'll eavesdrop on their conversations in the hopes of picking up something that might be useful later.

"He sounds angry, right?" Clothilde casts a glance toward the casket as she studies a woman I assume is the deceased's mother from up close. "Those screams aren't just panic."

We've become experts at interpreting screams. Every ghost screams. Who wouldn't when they wake up in a sealed casket? Only when the ghost accepts he is indeed a ghost will he be released into the cemetery. Some people need only hours, others weeks.

I screamed for five days, which is pretty close to average.

For every single arrival, I pray they'll be quick on the uptake because we have no way of escaping the screams. And listening to someone panic for weeks can be exhausting.

Clothilde is right, though. This guy is more angry than panicked. "Could be a murder victim," I say. "All the more reason to listen in." As I learned as a police officer and have observed as a dead ghost, the chances of his murderer being here are actually quite high.

I let Clothilde focus on the family members up front and wander over to what I assume to be a group of friends toward the back. Two dark-haired men in their late thirties, one blond woman who's obviously just the plus-one of one of the men, and one redhead who's fighting tears.

"I still don't understand why he was home that night," the redhead says, her eyes on the casket. "He was supposed to be in Thailand. They said he used his ticket. How did he even get back?"

The single guy shakes his head. "The police say his business was in trouble. He might have been up to something illegal and using the trip to Thailand as a cover." He sighs. "The fact that he was brutally murdered in what qualified as his office kind of supports their theory."

Definitely a murder case then. Which means our new friend will need for his murderer to get caught in order to find peace.

These cases are always the most difficult ones. Solving a murder while out in the real world is hard enough—doing it from the confines of a cemetery and without the possibility of interacting directly with anyone alive borders on impossible.

We've done it before, though.

"I heard they found proof it wasn't actually Henri on that plane to Thailand," the second man says while trying to free his hand from the death grip his wife has on it. "The images from the airport weren't top quality, but it seems like it was some sort of Henri lookalike."

"So Henri sent someone off as a decoy?" the first man says.

The redhead's lips wobble, but her eyes look angry. "That, or whoever killed Henri planned the whole thing out, and sent a lookalike so nobody would wonder where Henri was until the trail went cold."

Silence settles as the casket is being lowered into the ground.

Although I understand their wish to pay their respects to their friend, I need more information before they're all out of reach. Live people can't actually hear us when we talk, or feel us when we touch them. But there's something. Maybe their subconscious is able to hear what's going on on our side.

I don't know how it works, but I know it does. Sometimes, when we talk to the mourners, they…react to our nudges.

"Who would want to harm your friend?" I ask them. "Could it be linked to this business of his? Did he have any trouble with family members? Will someone benefit from his death?"

Asking a lot of questions in one go like this isn't optimal. The message might get jumbled, and I can end up with nothing. But I'm short on time, and I prefer throwing a wide net in the hopes of catching at least one fish.

"At least dealing with the estate should be easy," the married guy says. "There's nothing but the house, and from what I understand, the bank will take most of that. His brothers should each end up with about five thousand euros when everybody else have grabbed their share."

One motive ruled out.

"I hear Sylvie is furious," the redhead says, keeping her voice low.

All four gazes go to a woman with short dark hair standing alone just behind the family members.

"She'd been fighting with Henri about their business for months. She kept wanting to bring in a new accountant and Henri kept insisting on keeping the one they had because they couldn't afford one who wasn't a friend. Henri told me she was neglecting her parts of the business in favor of criticizing how he managed his."

The married guy sniffs. "Sounds like Sylvie, all right."

I manage to catch Clothilde's eye and point at Sylvie. "She appears to be a prime suspect. See if you can get something out of her?"

"Complicated if she's standing here all by herself," Clothilde yells back. "But all right." She strolls over to the woman and leans in so close their noses almost touch.

The casket is in the ground and the family seems to have said their goodbyes. People are going to start leaving.

"You think the police are going to find whoever killed him?" the single guy says.

"Not a chance." The redhead pulls her black shawl closer around her shoulders. "They have no clue who did it. They'll keep pretending to work the case, but they've clearly been going in circles for weeks already."

As the mourners start moving toward the parking lot, my group follows. I stick close, hoping they'll give me more information, but their conversation just turns to straight out police bashing and I learn nothing useful.

Clothilde catches up to us when we get close to the gate. "There was a guest hiding in one of the cypress trees. I saw one of the branches move and went over to check it out. Guy was getting a cramp." She waggles her eyebrows and her eyes twinkle. "He's definitely related to the dead guy. Looks like a younger, male version of the mourning mother."

Who cares about gossiping friends? A relative hiding in a cypress has a lot more potential.

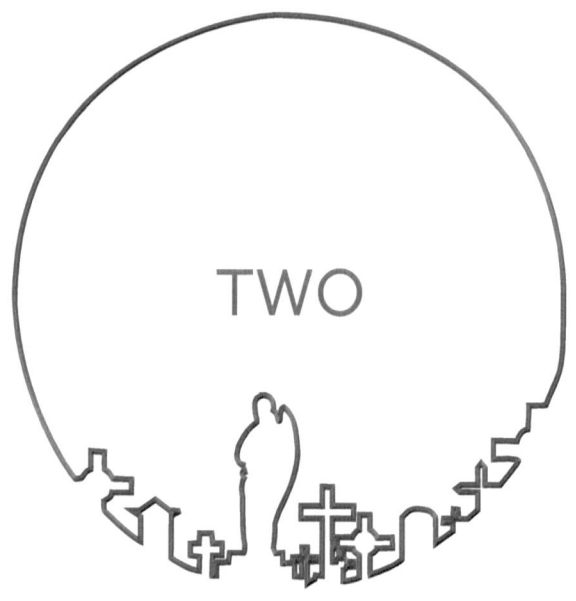

TWO

Clothilde is right. The guy climbing out of the cypress tree looks a lot like the grieving mother. There's something in the eyes and the set of his jaw.

"Did you hear talk of any family history?" I ask Clothilde. "Any estranged family member or someone getting criticized for not showing up?"

"No." Clothilde is standing at the foot of the tree, hands on hips, frowning at the man as he jumps down from the lowest branch. "From what I understood, Henri was an only child, so it can't be a brother. Maybe a cousin?"

"There has to be some family feud going on, or he'd participate like everybody else."

"Maybe he's a bastard brother." Clothilde lights up at the idea.

I grunt. "That might work if he looked like the father, not so much when it's the mother." Although I guess it's possible for women to have secret children, it's a lot more difficult for them to keep it a secret from their family. "Also, Henri was apparently thirty-seven, which must be pretty darn close to this guy's age."

"They were twins and the mother decided only to keep one?"

After a quick look to check he's still alone in the cemetery, the man takes off toward the back gate. He doesn't even glance at the fresh grave.

If he'd been here to actually mourn Henri, he would have gone over to pay his respects.

So why the hell is he here?

We have about three minutes before he's out the gate and out of our reach. "How are you related to Henri? Why did you hide in the tree? What are you afraid of?" I bombard him with questions, anything I can think of.

He's not going to answer, of course, unless he's extremely attuned to ghosts. But his subconscious might pick up on something, so I watch his face and his gait, hoping I'll see a tell if I hit on the right question.

I get nothing. His face stays calm and his pace unhurried. When he steps through the back gate, he walks over to an old sedan parked in the shade and drives away.

Clothilde and I are stuck at the gate.

The screams from Henri's grave continue.

THREE

It takes him five days to come to terms with his fate. On the fourth day, the screams become intermittent, during the night he starts knocking on the casket as if testing it for hollow spots, and the next morning, a hand breaks through the newly dug dirt, quickly followed by a head.

Clothilde and I have been waiting at the grave since yesterday. We like to be close whenever someone emerges from their grave. A welcome committee of sorts. Becoming a ghost can be a bit of a shock and I figure seeing a friendly face or two certainly won't do any harm.

"I'm returning to the secret child idea," Clothilde whispers when Henri's head bursts out of the ground.

No kidding. This guy looks nothing like his mother. Or father, for that matter. Both parents were blond, with blue or green eyes. The mother's eyes were set close together, which was what made the man in the tree resemble her so closely. This guy's eyes are brown and wide apart. His nose is kind of big, which was not a trait I saw in any of the other family members.

"Maybe he was adopted?" I whisper back. I stand up and put on a smile. Time for my welcome speech.

When Henri has figured out how to climb out of his grave and he spots us, I nod in greeting. "Hello there, and welcome to our cemetery. My name is Robert, and this here is Clothilde."

Henri frowns as he studies us each in turn, then nods back at me. "I'm Clément."

"Nice to Clément?"

"Yes." He frowns at me as if I'm stupid. "Clément Fontaine. We're all ghosts?"

This is where I usually start my spiel. Explain why he's a ghost, give some pointers on our cemetery, try to figure out what his unfinished business is.

But I'm mute. Can't get a single word out.

My gaze goes to the simple wooden cross that's used to mark the grave until the headstone is ready. It reads Henri Lambert.

Clothilde isn't faring much better. "Uh-oh," she whispers.

"What is wrong with you people—" The man's gaze follows ours. When he sees the name, he stops short. "What the...?"

"You're not Henri Lambert?" I have to ask.

"No." His voice is lighter, as if he's forgotten how to

breathe—which is odd, considering he doesn't need to breathe anymore.

"Well," Clothilde says. "At least that explains why none of the mourners looked anything like you."

I haven't needed to breathe in thirty years, but I'm sucking in air now. "But the guy in the tree did."

Clothilde's eyes widen. "You think that was Henri?"

"I don't know. Makes as much sense as anything else at this point. Does that mean Henri killed Clément? Did he kill someone else so everybody would think he was dead?"

My mind is about to explode. I plomp down on a nearby grave and bury my hands in my hair. How on earth are we going to figure this one out from the confines of the cemetery?

Although Clément initially seemed to have a pretty good grasp of how his ghostly body worked, he's now floating a foot off the ground and his pants have turned into shorts. He's as shocked by these revelations as we are.

"Nobody knows I'm dead? Or where I'm buried?"

"I guess not," I say with a wince. Then I pull myself together. I'm shocked by the revelation, but I'm not the one buried in the wrong grave—actually, I'm the one who doesn't even have a headstone, but that's a mystery for another day—so I have to be the strong one here. "Do you remember how you died?"

Clément shakes his head.

"What's the last thing you do remember?"

"Waking up inside the casket," Clément whispers.

Clothilde snorts and jumps up to perch on the grave next door. "That part does everyone in, don't worry. Try to focus on something nice from when you were alive. Like having breakfast. Or reading the newspaper. Something positive and focus on the last time you did it."

Feet now close to the ground but still wearing shorts, Clément frowns furiously as he tries to remember.

"I had breakfast at the hotel," he says slowly. "The croissant was stale but the coffee delicious."

"At a hotel?" I ask. "You're not from around here? Just outside Toulouse," I add when he starts looking around, searching for landmarks.

"I'm buried in Toulouse." The poor man looks completely lost. What seems to be a worn teddy bear makes a quick appearance in his right hand. "I'm from Lille," he whispers.

If he's buried on the other side of the country, his family has no chance of figuring out what happened to him.

So I guess we'll have to go at this from the Henri perspective. "It seems likely the reason you were killed was somehow linked to the guy whose name is on your grave." I straighten my spine and take on my police officer voice. Enough panicking, time to start figuring out what happened to this guy. "I'm fairly certain you were either killed by him or in his place. Anything else just doesn't make sense."

"So what do you remember after the stale croissant and good coffee?" Clothilde asks.

Seemingly over the worst of his shock, Clément sits down on the fresh dirt and recounts his last day among the living.

He was in Toulouse on business. He was a contractor and specialized in smart solutions for private homes. Although not for everyone, the people who did want smart houses were ready to pay a lot of money to have the latest technology manage menial tasks for them.

A company in Toulouse promised an interesting solution for making many different appliances work together. If his clients needed four different apps and three different remotes to manage their house, they weren't happy. This guy promised one app could deal with everything.

"This guy wasn't named Henri, by any chance?"

Clément shakes his head. "Bertrand Poulain. But I don't think I ever got so far as to meet with him."

Clothilde swings her legs through the gravestone she's sitting on. "The last hours before death tend to be a little hazy. Where were you meeting him?"

"At what passed for my office while I was in Toulouse," Clément says. "One of those coffee shop/office space things where you can rent a desk by the hour? I usually rent a desk for half a day when I'm traveling, so I'll have a place to work in peace and a place to receive clients and contractors. I don't like always going to them."

"And you remember arriving at the coffee shop?" I ask. I'm not familiar with the concept, but I get the essential idea.

"Yes." Clément nods. Then he frowns. "I do not remember leaving."

Clothilde looks my way and our gazes lock. "He was killed in the coffee shop office thingy?"

"Why would they mistake him for someone else then?" I turn back to Clément. "Do you give your name or show any kind of ID to get a spot?"

"Yes, my name would be in their system."

It's at times like these that I really miss being alive and able to leave the cemetery. What did the police learn at the coffee shop? How many other patrons were there? Did any of them have a connection with Henri or Clément? Was Henri there?

"Henri must have been there, too," I say out loud, as much to myself as to my companions. "If you were killed in that place and they mistook your body for his, he must have at least been scheduled to be there."

"I agree," Clothilde says. "Not that it helps us solve the case or anything. We're not getting anywhere until Henri/Clément here gets some visitors."

She's right, of course. But that doesn't mean we should just sit back and wait.

We have to prepare, so we know exactly what to do depending on who the visitor is.

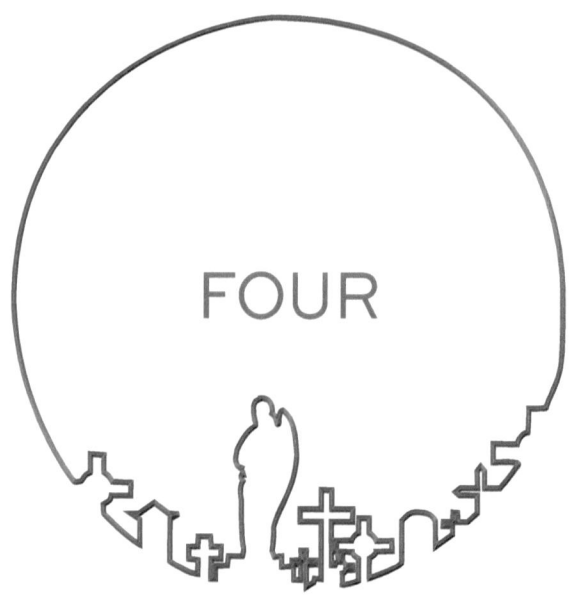

FOUR

THREE DAYS LATER, Henri's mother comes for a visit. She already came twice while Clément was still in the ground, but she never said anything coherent or interesting and at the time we didn't know what the deal was.

While I'm not at all certain she'll have any useful information for us, we're going to work her as best we can. The number of visitors significantly decreases after a couple of weeks.

Since Clothilde isn't the best with people over fifty, I'm the one who attempts to make contact with the woman as she kneels by what she thinks to be her son's grave. She has brought a single red rose to place on the grave.

"That's a beautiful rose," I tell her. "I'm sure your son would have appreciated it if he'd been the one to be buried here." I'm sitting cross-legged on the grave in front of her, watching for any sign that she hears me. "However, the problem is that the man who was buried here wasn't your son. Which should mean he's still alive and well out there somewhere, while you're mourning him here."

Her face is set in a frown, but it's no different from when she first came here. Of course a mother mourning her son won't be smiling. I'm not sure she's very sensitive to ghosts, which means I won't be getting through to her no matter what I do.

Still, I keep trying. I repeat over and over that her son isn't dead, that she should ask the police to reopen the case because clearly, mistakes were made.

She just kneels there as tears run down her cheeks.

I'm about to give up when Clément rushes up, eyes wide. "A guy came in through the back gate. Clothilde says it's Henri."

I jump up. "The guy in the tree?"

"That's what she said." Clément glances down at the kneeling woman. "She'd recognize her own son, right?"

"I would certainly hope so." God, we'd thought of so many different scenarios, but Henri coming back and running into his mother wasn't one of them. "Why would he come back here and run the risk of getting caught if he was the one to kill you?"

"I didn't recognize him." Clément hasn't been able to remember anything past arriving at the coffee shop, but seeing his murderer's face could have triggered a memory.

Maybe Henri didn't do it?

Leaving the mother behind, I rush after Clément toward the back gate.

The guy who'd been hiding in the tree during the funeral is playing James Bond in between the tombs. Crouching down, popping out his head to scope out the next stretch of gravel path before tiptoeing over to hide behind the next grave.

"I'm less and less convinced this guy is a criminal mastermind," Clothilde says. Arms crossed and lip curled, she'd probably have scared off poor Henri if he'd been able to see her three steps ahead of him.

I have to agree with her assessment. The only reason he hasn't been spotted is that the only live person in the cemetery is his mother, and she's busy crying her eyes out at his grave.

"We have to make sure she sees him," I say. "If the mother sees her son is alive, she'll realize they've buried the wrong person and Clément here can be exhumed and properly identified." At least I hope he will be. Somebody from Lille will have reported him missing by now.

"Clément, you go work on the mother. Tell her to look up from the grave, have a look around the cemetery. Clothilde and I will make sure Henri becomes visible."

Clément takes off with a quick salute and Clothilde and I get to work.

We're aiming for sensory overload. If we can speak loud enough to his subconscious, we might be able to override whatever his conscious brain is trying to think.

"You're not really hidden over there," Clothilde croons into his left ear. "Anybody can see you. You'd be much better off on the other side. Have you seen those houses over there? Lots of windows. I bet there are people looking for you and you're basically in plain sight."

"Your mother clearly misses you," I say into the right ear. "She's over there crying at what she thinks is your grave. Can you see her? Can you see her pain? That's because of you."

And on and on we go. Clothilde playing up his paranoia and me aiming for the heartstrings.

At first, it doesn't seem to work. He keeps moving from grave to grave, staying out of sight from his mother.

But then he throws a glance over his shoulder.

"Ah! Did you see the movement in that window over there?" Clothilde is having way too much fun with this. "I think someone saw you."

Henri steps around the grave he's hiding behind to stay out of sight of the nonexistent persons spying on him from the house. The movement puts him in sight of his mother.

Who unfortunately isn't looking in our direction.

But Henri is looking at her.

"See how sad she is?" I say. "You're the reason she's suffering, why she'll probably never again be truly happy. No parent really survives losing a son, you know."

I just wish I wasn't speaking from experience. After thirty years in this place, we've seen our fair share of grieving parents coming to their children's graves, and it's never a pretty sight. Henri may not be directly responsible for Clément's death, but he is responsible for his mother's pain.

I must be getting through somewhat because Henri has

stopped moving. He's staring at his mother, eyes wide and mouth working soundlessly.

And she still isn't looking up, despite Clément clearly trying his best.

"Oy!" Clothilde screams. "Lady! Over here!"

I jump a foot in the air, and even Henri seems startled. Then even more paranoid, when he can't figure out where the sound came from.

But more importantly, the mother looks up.

She recognizes her son instantly.

"Don't you dare run." Clothilde is practically growling into Henri's ear. "She knows you're alive now. You're not going to add insult to injury and disappear again."

He's on the verge or running anyway. But when his mother's incredulous cry sounds out across the cemetery, he caves.

Gulping loudly, he goes to meet his mother.

FIVE

Henri and his mother meet in the middle of the cemetery. The mother wraps her arms around him and squeezes him so hard he has trouble drawing breath.

Us ghosts settle in on the surrounding graves to watch the show. They don't need any more prodding at the moment.

"Henri, you're alive! How is this possible?" The mother pulls away only far enough to put one hand on her son's cheek. "You were dead. We buried you. How can you be alive?"

"Somebody else was buried in my place, Maman," Henri says. His voice is wobbly with emotion, but I'm not sure which one. "Some other guy was killed in my place. I was supposed to be at that table, because that's always my table, except that day somebody else booked it and I ended up in the corner booth instead."

Tears are streaming down the mother's face as her hand keeps touching her son's face to make sure he's actually there. "But my dear boy, why didn't you tell anybody it wasn't you? What kept you from speaking up? We thought we'd lost you!"

Ah, the beginnings of anger. I estimate Henri has two minutes max before he gets the talking to of a lifetime.

"The killer thought I was at my usual spot, too. He was after me, Maman! I heard him say my name before pulling the trigger. He said something about not knowing when to quit. Someone wants to kill me, Maman. I didn't want them to know they got the wrong guy, so I went out the back door and didn't dare come home."

"That was three weeks ago! Surely you could have found the time to tell your poor mother you were alive since then?"

The mother is no longer holding her son. Her hands are balled into fists at her sides as she glares up at him. "Or do you not care about your family at all? The pain of losing you is just something we should suffer because you're a coward?"

"Ouch," Clothilde says.

Clément sighs. "So it looks like I was killed for being in this guy's place at the wrong time? Great."

Dying for being in the wrong place at the wrong time is never easy to swallow. We've had a couple of these cases over the years, and generally, what they need to move on is to accept their fate in a c'est la vie kind of way. Clément isn't fading, though, despite apparently accepting the truth, so there must be something else he needs.

"I wanted to tell you!" Henri pleads with his mom. "But at first I assumed they would quickly discover I wasn't the guy who got his head blown off, so I decided to take what little extra time was given to me and go into hiding. Once the killer discovered I was alive, he'd come after me again!"

"What about Thailand?" the mother asks.

Henri has the decency to look shamefaced. "I sold it, along with my passport, to a guy evading arrest. I needed the money to save my business!"

The mother seems to decide she's going to let that one slide. She has enough to deal with. She glances at the fresh grave. "There's somebody else buried in there. The poor soul who was shot in your place."

"And I'd greatly appreciate it if you could inform the police of that fact," Clément shouts.

"Maman, somebody wants me dead!"

I'm going to assume Henri is too lost in his own panic to really see the look his mother sends him, or he'd have been running for the hills with his tail between his legs. "Which is why you have to go to the police, Henri! They can protect you. It's their job! Unless you were involved in something illegal? Even then! They don't condone murders, no matter who the victim is!"

"But…"

"Oh my God!" The mother throws her hands in the air and starts pulling her son toward the parking lot. "This is probably why they wanted to kill you, you know. Because that business of yours is on the verge of collapse and instead of admitting defeat, you let the misery drag on forever, just like you did when you were a kid. Sometimes, you just have to admit you failed and try something new!"

Although I'd love to listen in on this conversation for a while longer—this is the best entertainment we've had in years—they are about to pass through the gate and be out of our reach. And I need to make sure one message has come across.

"Please make sure to tell the police about the man who's actually buried here. His name is Clément, and his family doesn't know what happened to him."

Henri is still caught up in his self-pity, but the mother hears me. She looks over her shoulder toward the grave that was meant for her son and frowns. "We're going straight to the police, Henri. So that they can get the guy who wants to kill you, but also so that they can figure out who that poor soul is.

"You didn't only hurt your family with this nonsense, you hurt his too."

She pulls Henri toward his car like he's a screaming toddler, and two minutes later, it's just the three of us left in silence. Hoping the mother will come through on her promise.

SIX

Clément is understandably nervous as we wait for news. What if Henri convinces his mother that the danger is so great he should just stay in hiding? What if the mother's love for her son, and her fear of losing him again, outweighs her need for setting things right?

After all, they could let Henri stay officially dead and thereby keep him safe.

Which would leave Clément here, without any means of finding justice.

Although Clothilde and I have managed to solve a number of difficult cases over the years, figuring this one out without anyone who actually knew the victim ever showing up would be an impossible mission.

Three weeks after the visit, we're on the verge of giving up, when a team of gravediggers rolls into the parking lot, closely followed by a police car. The gravediggers' van is a fairly usual sight and could simply mean there's going to be a funeral soon, but the police car is not ordinary.

Two officers exit the car, and help a middle-aged, dark-haired woman out from the back seat.

"That's my mom." Clément sounds like he doesn't quite believe his eyes, and he's staying perfectly still where he's sitting on one of the cemetery's oldest tombs, as if worried the illusion will break if he moves.

"Henri's mother won through, then," Clothilde says from her perch on the next grave over. "No doubt about who has the balls in that family. You think Henri is at home, hiding under his bed?"

I chuckle. "My bet is on filing for bankruptcy. That's what the killer wanted, right? So if he officially goes out of business, there should be no more reason to kill him."

There's a chance we'll never know what happened to Henri, and that's just fine with me. He's not the one I'm responsible for—Clément is. Henri has his mom to get his act together and set the police on the tracks of the killer.

I have an hour, max, to help Clément figure out what his unfinished business is.

"Once your casket leaves the cemetery, you'll go with it," I tell him. "You'll be stuck wherever your body is. You need to figure out what your unfinished business is and deal with it. Then it won't matter where your body is, you'll move on to a better place."

Clément is barely listening as he walks pretty much inside one of the police officers holding his mother up, so he can stay close to her.

"If what you need is to find your killer, you'll want to convince your mother to come visit your grave often so she can give you updates."

"I don't care about the killer," Clément says absently. "He wasn't after me, so if he gets caught or not doesn't really change anything for me. I'm dead either way."

Seeing the way he looks at his mother makes it clear just how different Clément and Henri are. One couldn't be bothered to tell his mother he was alive, while the other is clearly worried how his mother will take his passing away. "Maybe what you need is simply to say goodbye properly to your loved ones," I say. "For them to know what happened to you."

Clément's mother has reached the grave, where the gravediggers are already at work. The two police officers, one looking a little green around the gills from having a ghost inside him for the last five minutes, bring her to a bench farther down the path, so she can watch as they exhume her son.

Once they move away, Clément starts talking to his mother. "I'm so sorry you have to go through this, Maman. I know you always told us we weren't allowed to die before you. But I'm fine now that you'll bring me home to Lille, I promise."

It's difficult to tell if he's getting through. She doesn't show any outward sign of reacting…except she might be a little calmer already.

"You can talk to him, you know," Clothilde says. "Talk to the casket. He can hear you."

Clément turns to glare at Clothilde, apparently annoyed by the interruption.

But then the mother starts talking. "You weren't supposed to go before me, Clément. You knew that." Tears are forming at the corners of her eyes, but she's fighting to keep them from falling. "A mother isn't supposed to bury her son. Or discover he's already been buried in somebody else's grave because the police aren't capable of doing their jobs."

"I'm so sorry, Maman," Clément repeats as he's doing his best to hold his mother's hands where they're folded in her lap.

"I shouldn't have put that kind of pressure on you, though," the mother continues. "Who knows if you'll find peace with the way I've been hounding you all your life to stay alive longer than me. I didn't mean that so literally, son."

"What do you mean?" Clément whispers.

"You and your brothers were so wild when you were younger. Doing crazy thing after crazy thing, giving me heart attacks left and right. Forcing you to worry about me was the only thing that seemed to work to get you to calm down." She sighs. "And here you are, getting killed for working in some other man's spot, through no fault of your own."

Hoping Clément won't mind, I ask the one question I need answered. "How did they know it's Clément in there before exhuming the body?"

I expect another annoyed look from Clément, but he seems too shaken by his mother's words to even notice my interruption.

The mother glances around the cemetery, not really looking at anything. "After that other man showed up alive and kicking, it didn't take the police more than thirty minutes to figure out what happened, you know. One call to that coffee shop and they realized somebody else had paid for his spot that day." A shuddering sigh. "And that someone was reported missing two days after the murder. I guess it's possible it's not you they're going to find in there."

"It's me, Maman," Clément says.

I try to signal to Clothilde. I think Clément is turning transparent. Could this talk with his mother really be everything he needs?

"But I know it's you," the mother says. "I can feel it in my bones. Just like I can feel you're worried about me." She takes a deep breath and straightens her back. "So you listen to me one last time, chéri. Don't you worry about your mother. Your brothers will take care of me. You worry about yourself, and figure out how to find peace, all right? You've deserved it."

He's definitely on his way. He isn't much more than an outline as he clutches his mother's hands. Usually, I say goodbye to ghosts as they move on, but this time I refrain. He doesn't seem to realize what is happening, and I think being with his mother during his last moments is exactly what he needs.

Two minutes later, as the casket is lifted out of the grave, Clément is gone.

"It's a shame," Clothilde says with a lopsided smile. "Now we'll never know what it's like to haunt a plane."

I grin but don't say anything. There's one more thing we need to do here today.

"Your son has found peace," I tell Clément's mother. "You being here and saying the right words helped him move on."

There's no way to know if she heard me, but I'd like to think the nod she gives the casket as it is transported out of the cemetery means she got the message.

And the way her head is held high as she follows in its wake gives me hope she will survive without her son.

Then it's just the two of us left. Clothilde perching on her gravestone and me lounging on my bump on the ground. Waiting for new ghosts to help and working on our own redemption.

ABOUT THE AUTHOR

R.W. WALLACE WRITES in most genres, though she tends to end up in mystery more often than not. Dead bodies keep popping up all over the place whenever she sits down in front of her keyboard.

The stories mostly take place in Norway or France; the country she was born in and the one that has been her home for two decades. Don't ask her why she writes in English—she won't have a sensible answer for you.

Her Ghost Detective short story series appears in *Pulphouse Magazine*, starting in issue #9.

You can find all her books, long and short, all genres, on rwwallace.com.

Also by R.W. Wallace

Mystery

Ghost Detective Novels
Beyond the Grave
Unveiling the Past
Beneath the Surface
Piercing the Veil

Ghost Detective Shorts
Just Desserts
Lost Friends
Family Bonds
Common Ground
Till Death
Family History
Heritage
New Beginnings
Far From Home
Severed Ties
Eternal Bond
Harsh Expectations
Dull Expectations

Ghost Detective Collections
Unfinished Business, Volume 1
Unfinished Business, Volume 2

The Tolosa Mystery Series
The Red Brick Haze
The Red Brick Cellars
The Red Brick Basilica

SHORT STORY COLLECTIONS
Deep Dark Secrets
A Thief in the Night

ROMANCE

FRENCH OFFICE ROMANCE SERIES
Flirting in Plain Sight
Hiding in Plain Sight

STANDALONE NOVELS
Love at First Flight

HOLIDAY STORIES

COLLECTIONS
Heartwarming Holiday Tales

SHORT STORIES
The Case of the Disappearing Gingerbread City
Crooks and Nannies

YOUNG ADULT SHORT STORY COLLECTIONS

Tales From the Trenches

Find all R.W. Wallace's books:

rwwallace.com/allbooks

www.ingramcontent.com/pod-product-compliance
Lightning Source LLC
LaVergne TN
LVHW040203080526
838202LV00042B/3306